Princess Mirror-Belle and the Magic Shoes

Julia Donaldson

Illustrated by Lydia Monks

MACMILLAN CHILDREN'S BOOKS

First published 2005 by Macmillan Children's Books
a division of Macmillan Publishers Limited
20 New Wharf Road, London N1 9RR
Basingstoke and Oxford
www.panmacmillan.com
Associated companies throughout the world

ISBN 0 330 43329 6

Text copyright © Julia Donaldson 2005
Illustrations copyright © Lydia Monks 2005

The right of Julia Donaldson and Lydia Monks to be identified as the
author and illustrator of this work has been asserted by them in accordance
with the Copyright, Designs and Patents Act 1988.

3 5 7 9 8 6 4 2

A CIP catalogue record for this book is available from
the British Library.

Printed and bound in Great Britain by Mackays of Chatham plc, Kent

For Alyssa and Brooke

Contents

Chapter One

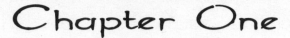

The Magic Shoes

"Hey, you! Yes, you! Turn around, look over your shoulder," sang Ellen's brother, Luke, into the microphone.

Ellen was sitting in the village hall watching Luke's band, Breakneck, rehearse for the Battle of the Bands. The hall was nearly empty, but that evening it would be packed with fans of the six different bands who were entering the competition.

As well as being Breakneck's singer, Luke wrote most of their songs, including this one.

"It's me! Yes, me! Turn around, I'm

still here," he sang. Then he wandered moodily around the stage, while the lead guitarist, Steph, played a twangy solo.

Steph, who never smiled, wore frayed baggy black trousers with a pointless chain hanging out of the pocket and a black T-shirt with orange flames on it. The solo went on and on.

"Steph's so good at the guitar," Ellen whispered to Steph's sister Seraphina, who was sitting next to her.

"I know," said Seraphina. She was two years older than Ellen and dressed very much like her brother, except that her T-shirt had a silver skull on it. "But I bet they don't win. I don't think they should have chosen this song. It's not going to get people dancing. Steph wrote a much better one called 'Savage'.

Ellen couldn't imagine Steph writing anything dancy, but she was quite shy of Seraphina and didn't say so. Besides, she had just remembered something.

"Dancing – help! I'm going to be late for ballet!" She picked up a bag from the floor.

"You've got the wrong bag – that's mine," said Seraphina, who also went to ballet, but to a later class.

"Sorry." Ellen grabbed her own bag and hurried to the door.

At least she didn't have far to go. The ballet classes were held in a room called the studio, which was above the hall. Ellen ran up the stairs.

The changing room was empty. The other girls must be in the studio already, but Ellen couldn't hear any music so the class couldn't have started yet.

Hurriedly, she put on her leotard and ballet shoes and scooped her hair into the hairnet that Madame Jolie, the ballet teacher, insisted they all wear. Madame Jolie was very fussy about how they looked and could pounce on a girl for the smallest thing, such as crossing the ribbons on her ballet shoes in the wrong way.

Ellen was just giving herself a quick check in the full-length mirror when a voice said, "What's happened to your feet?"

It was a voice that she knew very well.

It was coming from the mirror and it belonged to Princess Mirror-Belle.

Ellen and Mirror-Belle had met several times before. Mirror-Belle looked just like Ellen's reflection, but instead of staying in the mirror as reflections usually do, she had a habit of coming out of it. She was much cheekier and naughtier than Ellen and she was always boasting about her life in the palace and the magic things that she said happened to her.

Ellen hadn't seen Mirror-Belle for a while, and she wasn't sure how pleased she was to see her now. All too often Mirror-Belle had got them both into trouble and then escaped into a mirror, leaving Ellen to take the blame.

"Mirror-Belle! You can't come to my dancing class," she said now, then added, "What do you mean about my feet anyway? What's wrong with them?"

"They're not dancing!" said Princess

Mirror-Belle, leaping out of the mirror into the changing room. She was wearing an identical leotard and ballet shoes to Ellen's, and a hairnet too, though she pulled this off and flung it to the ground with a shudder, saying, "I must have walked through a spider's web." Then she began to prance around the room, pointing her toes and waving her arms.

"Stop! You'll tire yourself out before the class has even started," said Ellen.

"I can't stop. And I'm surprised that you can. I think you should take your shoes back to the elves and complain."

"What elves?" asked Ellen.

But already Mirror-Belle had opened the door to the studio and was dancing in. Ellen followed her with a sinking feeling.

The other girls in the class were standing in a line, waiting to curtsy to Madame Jolie. Ellen and Mirror-Belle joined the line. Some of the girls tittered as Mirror-Belle continued to dance up and down on the spot.

"Who's she?" asked one.

"She looks just like you, Ellen," said another.

Madame Jolie had been talking to the lady who played the piano, but now she turned round to face the class.

"*Bonjour, mes élèves*," she said.

This meant "Good day, my pupils," in

French. Madame Jolie was French and she always started the class like this.

"*Bonjour, Madame*," chanted Ellen and the other girls as they dropped a curtsy to the teacher – all except Mirror-Belle, who twirled around with her arms above her head.

"Leetle girl on ze left – zat ees not a curtsy," said Madame Jolie.

"Ah, you noticed – well done." Mirror-

Belle jiggled about as she spoke. "No, I *never* curtsy – except very occasionally to my parents, the King and Queen. And I'm surprised that all these girls are curtsying to you instead of to me – or are you a princess too?"

"Zees ees not ze comedy class," replied Madame. Then her frown deepened. "Where ees your 'airnet?" she asked.

"A *hairnet*, did you say? Why on earth should I wear one of those? The only thing I ever put on my head is a crown. I didn't wear one today, though, because . . ." Mirror-Belle paused for a second and then went on, "because one of the diamonds fell out of it yesterday and it had to go to the palace jeweller to be repaired."

Ellen wondered if this was true. She had never seen Mirror-Belle with a crown on and sometimes doubted if she really *was* a princess.

"If you forget ze 'airnet one more time you will leave ze class," warned Madame. Then she ordered the girls to go to the barre.

"We will practise ze *pliés*. First position, everyone."

Ellen and the others held the barre with their right hands and, with their heels together, turned their toes out. Then, as the piano started up, they all bent their knees and straightened up again. Ellen couldn't see Mirror-Belle, who was behind her, but she could hear a thumping sound and some stifled giggles.

"*Non, non, non!*" exclaimed Madame. She clapped her hands to stop the music and then wagged her finger at Mirror-Belle. "Why ees it zat you are jumping? I said plié, not sauté. A plié is a bend. A sauté is a jump." She demonstrated the two movements gracefully.

"It's no use telling me that," said Mirror-Belle, leaving the barre and dancing up to Madame. "It's my ballet shoes you should be talking to."

Some of the girls giggled, but Madame was not impressed. "Do not argue, and keep still!" she ordered Mirror-Belle.

"But I can't!" Mirror-Belle complained. "I did think that *you* might understand about my shoes, even if Ellen doesn't. I can see I'll have to explain."

"Zere is no need for zat," said Madame, but Mirror-Belle ignored her. Skipping around in time to her own words, she said, "They're magic shoes. As soon as I put them on, my feet start dancing and I can't stop till the soles are worn out." She twirled around and then added, "Sometimes I dance all night."

"Then why aren't they worn out already?" asked one of the girls, and received a glare from Madame.

"This is a new pair," said Mirror-Belle. "Some elves crept into the palace and made them for me in the night. I hid behind a curtain and watched them. Luckily they didn't see me. If they found out I knew about them, they'd probably never come back. They're very shy, you see." She leaped in the air and landed with a thump. "This pair is very well made. They'll probably take ages to wear out."

Madame had had enough. "In zat case, you can go and wear zem out somewhere else," she said angrily.

"What a good idea," said Mirror-Belle. "So you're not just a pretty pair of feet after all," and she flitted and twirled her way to the door.

"Come on, Ellen!" she called over her shoulder as she danced out of the room.

Ellen hesitated. Part of her wanted to follow Mirror-Belle, to try to stop her causing too much chaos elsewhere. On the other hand, she never was very good at that; usually she just got drawn into whatever trouble Mirror-Belle created. She decided to stay where she was. With a bit of luck, Mirror-Belle might get bored and go back through the changing-room mirror into her own world.

"What an *enfant terrible*!" muttered Madame. "And no 'airnet!" she added, as if this was the worst crime of all. Then she turned back to the class. "Now, *mes élèves*, we will do ze *pliés* in second position."

Ellen's mother, Mrs Page, was teaching the piano to Robert Rumbold when the doorbell rang.

"Excuse me, Robert," she said, interrupting a piece called "Boogie Woogie Bedbug", which Robert was playing very woodenly. She went to the door.

"Ellen, you're back very early – and why are you still in your dancing things?"

"I'm not Ellen, I'm Princess Mirror-Belle," said the girl on the doorstep. She danced past Ellen's mother and into the sitting room.

"Don't be silly, Ellen. And come out of there. You know you're not allowed in the sitting room when I'm teaching."

Ellen's mother had never met Mirror-Belle before. Although Ellen was always talking about her, her mother thought she was just an imaginary friend.

Robert was still playing "Boogie Woogie Bedbug", and the girl who Mrs Page thought was Ellen was slinking around the room, waggling her hips and clicking her fingers in time to the music.

"You heard me, Ellen. Go to your room and get changed. Where are your clothes anyway?"

"That's a tricky question. It depends on whether my maid is having a lazy day or not. If she is, then my clothes are still on the palace floor where  I left them. If she's not, then they're hanging up in the royal wardrobe," said the girl, jumping on to the sofa and off again.

"I suppose you've left them at ballet," said Mrs Page with a sigh. "You'd better go back there now and get changed."

"That's really no way to talk to a princess, but since you're my friend's mother I'll excuse you." She danced out of the room and Ellen's mother heard the front door slam.

"I'm so sorry about that, Robert," she said.

Robert just grunted and went on playing "Boogie Woogie Bedbug". Strangely enough, the piece was now sounding much livelier than before, as if the bedbug had learned to jump at last.

"That's coming on so much better," Mrs Page told him as she saw him out a few minutes later. "Keep practising it, and then next week you can start on 'Hip Hop Hippo'."

Just then she spotted Ellen coming round the corner towards the house. She was wearing her outdoor clothes.

"Hello, Ellen – that was very quick! You're back just in time to apologize to Robert."

"What for?" asked Ellen, looking puzzled.

"For barging in to his lesson like that."

"Oh no, don't say Mirror-Belle's been here," groaned Ellen. "Where is she now?"

"She's in your imagination – just the same as usual – so stop blaming her for everything you do wrong. In fact, if you mention Mirror-Belle one more time I won't let you go to the Battle of the Bands."

That evening Ellen, who had succeeded in not mentioning Mirror-Belle (though she kept thinking about her), was standing near the front of the village hall waiting for the second half of the Battle of the Bands to start. Three of the bands had played already, and the last of these, Hellhole, had received wild applause. Breakneck would have to play really well to beat them.

"Do you want a Coke?" came a voice. It was Seraphina, who had pushed her way through the crowds of people to join Ellen.

"Thanks. I like your T-shirt – it's cool," said Ellen.

Seraphina was no longer wearing her skull T-shirt. This one had a green-winged snake on it.

"Did you hear what happened to my other one?" asked Seraphina. "It was stolen from the changing room while I was at my ballet class. So were my jeans. Who do you think could have taken them?"

"I've no idea," said Ellen untruthfully.

In fact, she had a very strong suspicion. Mirror-Belle must have danced back to the hall while the older girls were having their lesson and changed into Seraphina's black jeans and silver-skull T-shirt. But where was she now?

Just then the lights in the hall were dimmed and some bright-coloured ones came on over the stage.

"Hi there, pop-pickers! Welcome back to the battlefield!" said the compère, Mr Wilks, who was a geography teacher in Luke's school.

Seraphina sniggered. "He's not exactly cool, is he?" she whispered.

Ellen decided she didn't like the superior way in which Seraphina always spoke. Mirror-Belle put on airs too, but at least she could be good fun. Ellen wondered again where she had got to.

"Put your paws together for Breakneck!" said Mr Wilks, and Ellen clapped much louder than anyone else as Luke, Steph and the other members of Breakneck slouched on to the stage.

Luke tripped up on his way to his place and everyone laughed. Ignoring them, he hunched over the microphone.

"Hey, you! Yes, you!" he began.

He was pointing at the audience, and Ellen thought he looked quite good, but she could hear him only very faintly. Then he stopped altogether and signalled to Steph and the others to stop playing. What had gone wrong?

The sound technician came on to the stage, sighed and plugged the lead from Luke's microphone into the amplifier.

"It must have come unplugged when he tripped," said Seraphina.

Not looking too put out, Luke started again.

"Hey, you! Yes, you!

Turn around, look over your shoulder," he sang.

A loud screeching sound accompanied his voice.

"Feedback," whispered Seraphina knowledgeably.

This time, Luke didn't stop. The sound technician fiddled about with a knob and soon Luke's voice sounded normal. In fact, he was singing really well, Ellen thought, though she probably wouldn't admit it to him afterwards. But it had not been a good beginning. Some of the audience were still laughing, and a couple of Hellhole fans tried to start up a chant of, "Get them off!"

Breakneck didn't let any of this upset them. They carried on, and by the time Steph's twangy guitar solo started quite a few people were tapping their feet and swaying. The coloured lights were flashing and some smoke started to rise from the foot of the stage.

"That's the smoke machine," said

Seraphina. "It was Steph's idea."

The guitar solo came to an end at last and Luke started the "Hey, you!" chorus again.

Ellen was aware of a disturbance somewhere behind her.

"Watch out!"

"Stop pushing!"

"That was my toe!"

She turned around and saw who was creating the fuss and bother. It was a girl dressed in black, dancing her way through the crowds. Because she was flinging her arms around, people were making way for her and soon she was at the very front of the hall.

"Turn around," sang Luke, and the girl turned around, her loose hair flying about.

"Look over your shoulder," he sang, and she stuck her chin out over her right shoulder, at the same time stamping her

** 23 **

right foot and raising her left hand. Her wild hair was almost covering her face, but Ellen had no doubt who it was.

"Mirror-Belle, how could you?" she muttered under her breath. Just when Breakneck were beginning to impress people . . . This would ruin their chances!

But, to her surprise, a couple of girls in the front row started copying Mirror-Belle's movements, turning around whenever she did, looking over their shoulders with the same stamp and hand gesture, and pointing whenever Luke sang "Hey, you!" Some people stared at them, but others began to join in.

The dance was infectious. Very soon nearly everyone in front of Ellen seemed to be doing it. They were joining in the words of the song as well. She turned round and saw that the people behind her were dancing and singing too.

On the stage, Luke was grinning. He

caught Steph's eye and mouthed something to him. Ellen knew that they were at the end of the song, but they weren't slowing down like they usually did.

"They've gone back to the beginning! They're going to sing it all over again!" she whispered to Seraphina happily.

She expected Seraphina to look happy too, but instead she was staring accusingly at Mirror-Belle.

"Have you seen what I have?" she asked. "She's wearing my clothes! She's the thief!"

She strode forward, pushing through the dancers in front of her and reaching out for the skull T-shirt, which looked more like a dress on Mirror-Belle. Just when Seraphina tried to grab it,

Mirror-Belle did another of her spins
and, for the first time,
noticed Ellen behind
her.

"Oh, hello, Ellen.
Why didn't you come
with me? I've been vis-
iting your local library.
It hasn't got nearly so
many books as the
palace library, but that's
quite good in a way,
because it meant there
was lots of room for danc-
ing about. I must say, though, some of
the servants in there are awfully rude."

So that's where Mirror-Belle had been!
Now Ellen would dread going to the
library, knowing that the librarians
would think she was the naughty dancing
girl they had told off.

Meanwhile, the rest of the audience

were so carried away with the song and dance that they didn't spot that Mirror-Belle had stopped doing the actions along with them. They took no more notice of her – apart from Seraphina, that is, who was making another grab at the T-shirt.

Mirror-Belle was too quick for her. "Excuse me," she said, "my shoes are taking off again!" and the next moment she was dancing her way back through the crowds.

Seraphina followed her, and Ellen followed Seraphina. The rest of the audience just went on dancing in time to the music – almost as if they were all wearing magic shoes themselves.

"Where's she gone?"

asked Seraphina.

They were out of the hall now and Mirror-Belle was nowhere to be seen.

"Let's look outside," suggested Ellen.

In fact, she was pretty sure that Mirror-Belle would be on her way to the nearest mirror, the one in the changing room upstairs, but she wanted to give her a little time to escape from Seraphina. She felt a bit guilty about this – after all, Mirror-Belle had taken Seraphina's clothes – but she couldn't help being on Mirror-Belle's side.

They peered out of the front door and up and down the street.

"No," said Seraphina. "Anyway, she wouldn't go outside – she was wearing ballet shoes."

You don't know Mirror-Belle, thought Ellen, but said nothing.

"Let's look upstairs," said Seraphina, and she led the way.

"Look! There are my clothes on the floor!" she cried, as they entered the changing room. She picked them up. "They're drenched in sweat!" she said in disgust. "You'd think she'd been dancing ever since she put them on. Here, you hold them, Ellen – I'm going to find her."

Seraphina strode into the studio, but emerged a few moments later, looking puzzled. "That's funny," she said. "She's not in there, and there's no other way out." Then, "Why are you smiling?" she asked Ellen, who was glancing at the mirror.

Ellen didn't want to tell Seraphina that she knew where Mirror-Belle had gone. She would have to explain her smile some other way.

"I'm smiling," she said, "because I'm sure Breakneck are going to win the Battle of the Bands."

Then she turned back to the mirror

and quietly, so that Seraphina wouldn't hear, she whispered, "Thanks, Mirror-Belle."

Chapter Two

The Golden Goose

"Ooh, look, here comes Dad! Now he's off again – that was quick!" Ellen's granny sounded very excited. She was peering out of the window of the spare bedroom through a pair of binoculars. "He'll be back again in no time, you wait and see . . . Yes, here he is! Good old Dad!"

Granny wasn't talking about Ellen's father, who was away in Paris with her mother, but about a blue tit that was flying in and out of a nesting box in the garden, feeding his young family.

"Here, you have a look, Ellen!"

Granny passed over the binoculars and Ellen trained them on the nesting box, which was hanging from a tree. Sure enough, she saw the little bird fly in through the hole in the box and then out again.

"Keep watching! I'll go and make the tea," said Granny.

Ellen watched the blue tit come and go a few times, then lost interest and started experimenting with the binoculars. She found that if she looked through them the other way round, the tree with the nesting box appeared very small and far away. Everything did. She turned slowly round the bedroom, looking through the binoculars at the tiny bed, chest of drawers and wardrobe. It looked like a bedroom in a doll's house.

"And I'm the doll," she said, peering at her own shrunken reflection in the wardrobe mirror.

"Don't you mean the elephant?" came an answering voice, and out of the mirror jumped a tiny girl with a tiny pair of binoculars of her own. Although she was so small, Ellen recognized her immediately. It was Princess Mirror-Belle.

"Mirror-Belle! You've shrunk!" Removing the binoculars from her eyes, Ellen squatted down to talk to Princess Mirror-Belle, who had climbed on to her shoe.

"Don't be silly – it's you who've grown," replied Mirror-Belle, adding, "I must say, I'm surprised to find you here at all. What

are you doing at the top of a beanstalk?"

"I'm not at the top of a beanstalk," said Ellen. She was about to tell Mirror-Belle that she was at her grandparents' house, staying there for the Easter weekend, when a gruff voice called out, "Ellen! It's teatime!"

"It's the giant!" cried Mirror-Belle, clutching Ellen's ankle in alarm.

"No, it's not – it's Grandpa," said Ellen.

Mirror-Belle took no notice. "You'll have to hide me, Ellen!" she said.

"Oh, all right," said Ellen. "How about in here?" She picked Mirror-Belle up carefully and popped her into the drawer of the bedside table.

"It's much too hard," complained Mirror-Belle. "Not at all suitable for a princess. Can't you line it with velvet, or moss, or something?"

Ellen looked around. There was a box

of tissues on the table. She pulled out a few. "Will these do?" she asked as she set them down in the drawer. Mirror-Belle looked doubtful, but when Grandpa's voice came again – "Ellen! Hurry up!" – she lay down on the tissues.

"Don't forget *my* tea, will you?" she said, as Ellen went out of the room. "Beanstalk-climbing is hungry work."

There were home-made scones for tea. Ellen wanted to sneak one into her pocket for Mirror-Belle, but it was difficult to find the right moment. Granny and Grandpa never seemed to take their attention off her: they kept talking to her about their two favourite subjects – the garden and the birds who visited it.

"Over four hundred daffodils we had this year," said Granny. And, "Wait till you see my new bird bath, Ellen," boasted Grandpa.

It was only when Granny called out, "Look! There they are, the rascals!" that both their heads turned to the window to look at a pair of magpies, and Ellen whisked the scone off her plate and into her pocket.

It was a while before she could give it to Mirror-Belle, since Grandpa insisted on taking her on a tour of the garden first, pointing out with pride the bird bath and the gnomes, which he had carved himself. When Ellen eventually managed to escape to her bedroom, she found Princess Mirror-Belle in a grumpy mood.

"Not very appetizing," she said, giving the scone a disapproving look.

"It's delicious," said Ellen, and broke it into crumbs.

Mirror-Belle seized a handful of crumbs and stuffed them into her mouth. "The palace pastry-cook would get the sack if he produced anything as plain as this," she grumbled, but she ate all the crumbs swiftly and they seemed to improve her mood. "Now," she said, "it's time to look for the golden goose."

"What golden goose?" asked Ellen.

"The one that lays the golden eggs, of course. A giant stole it from the palace and I've come to get it back. I wonder where he's hidden it." Mirror-Belle picked up her tiny binoculars and put them to her eyes the wrong way round.

"You need to look through the other end for spotting birds," said Ellen.

Mirror-Belle looked put out for a second, but then retorted, "I cer-  tainly do not. Everything here is terrifyingly huge already. If I made it look any bigger I'd probably die of fright. This is giant land, remember."

Ellen laughed. "Do you think

I'm a giant then?" she asked.

"That's been puzzling me," said Mirror-Belle. "No. I think that the giants must have been fattening you up to eat you. But don't worry, I know how to make a special shrinking potion. Could you get hold of some petrol and shoe polish, and a few spoonfuls of marmalade?"

"*No*," said Ellen. "It would just get me into trouble, like that time in the bathroom."

She was remembering the very first time they had met. Mirror-Belle had appeared out of the bathroom mirror and persuaded Ellen to mix up all sorts of things in the bath.

Mirror-Belle looked slightly disappointed but then said, "While we're on the subject of baths, it's about time that I had mine." She yawned, and added, "And then bed, I think. We can always hunt for the golden goose tomorrow."

So Mirror-Belle was planning to stay the night! Ellen wasn't sure how she felt about that. Still, a bath couldn't do any harm. Ellen pointed to the washbasin in the corner of the bedroom. "Will you have your bath in there?" she asked.

"Good heavens, no!" said Mirror-Belle. "It's the size of the palace swimming pool. Surely you could find me something more suitable." She looked around and then pointed out of the window. "That coconut shell would be just the job. I can't think why it's hanging from a tree."

"I can't get you that," said Ellen. "It's got fat and raisins and things in it, for the birds."

A suspicious look crossed Mirror-Belle's face at the mention of birds. "For the golden goose, perhaps?" she said.

Ellen decided to change the subject back to Mirror-Belle's bath. "I've got a different idea," she said, and left the room.

She tiptoed past the sitting room, where Granny and Grandpa were watching television, and into the kitchen. In a cupboard she found a pretty china sugar bowl with a pattern of bluebells on it. It wasn't the one Granny used every day, and Ellen hoped she wouldn't miss it.

Mirror-Belle was delighted with her flowery china bath. "It's almost as good

as the one in the palace, which has roses and lilies on it," she said. She splashed around happily, and allowed herself to be dried with Ellen's face flannel. Then, "What about my nightdress?" she asked.

"I suppose you'll just have to get back into your clothes," said Ellen, but Mirror-Belle would hear of no such thing. "Can't you make one for me out of rose petals?" she said.

"No," said Ellen. "It's not the time of year for roses, and I'm no good at sewing. Granny is, though," she added, suddenly remembering the clothes-peg dolls she used to play with when she was little, and the dresses Granny made for them.

The dolls used to be kept in an old wooden toy box under the spare-room bed. Ellen knelt down and looked. Yes! The box was still there; she recognized its brass handles. She pulled it out and rummaged inside, while Mirror-Belle shivered and said, "Do hurry up! I'm freezing!"

At the bottom of the box Ellen found the five clothes-peg dolls. She took them out and lifted Mirror-Belle down to the floor to show them to her. Four of the dolls had quite plain cotton dresses, but the fifth had a shiny purple one; Ellen remembered Granny making it from a silk tie that Grandpa didn't like.

Mirror-Belle's eyes lit up and she practically ripped the purple dress off the doll, then pulled it over her own head.

"Now, all that remains to be found is the royal bed," she said. "And I think I've spotted it." She ran under the big bed and climbed into one of Ellen's slippers. "I don't expect the giants will look for me here," she said.

"Would you like one of my socks as a sleeping bag?" asked Ellen, who was beginning to enjoy herself. It was a bit like having the very latest walkie-talkie doll to play with, even though Mirror-Belle was rather a bossy doll. Ellen actually felt disappointed when Granny called her away for a game of cards.

"Don't forget my cocoa!" Mirror-Belle
called out after her, but when
Ellen came back to the bedroom she was fast
asleep.

The following
morning Mirror-
Belle announced that she was going to
search high and low for the golden goose.
"It's a good thing I've got you to help me,
Ellen," she said. "You can look in all the
high-up places."

But Ellen had other plans for the day:
Granny and Grandpa had promised to
take her out to the local safari park.

Mirror-Belle looked sulky when she
heard this, but then her face brightened.
"I suppose it's quite cunning of you to get
the giants out of the way, so that I can
carry out my search in peace," she said.

Ellen began to worry. "You're not to

mess up the house," she warned Mirror-Belle. "And what will you eat and drink all day?"

"You'll have to see to that," said Mirror-Belle. "Whoever heard of a princess getting her own meals?"

Ellen managed to scrounge a few bits of food before she set out with Granny and Grandpa: some Choc-o-Hoops from her own breakfast, a scraping of cheese from the sandwiches Granny was making for their picnic and a couple of grapes from the fruit bowl. She delivered them to Mirror-Belle on a tray that was really the lid of a jam jar, and filled

the cap of her shampoo bottle with water.

"I'd prefer cowslip cordial," said Mirror-Belle.

"Tough," said Ellen, surprising herself by answering back for once. Maybe it was easier than usual because Mirror-Belle was so much smaller than her. Feeling a bit guilty, she said, "I'll try and save you some goodies from the picnic."

Ellen enjoyed the safari park, but she couldn't help worrying what Mirror-Belle might be getting up to. She wished now that she had been hard-hearted enough to close her bedroom door before setting out.

"I'll put the kettle on," said Granny when they got back.

Ellen ran up to her bedroom, feeling relieved that the hall and stairs at least looked the same as when they had left.

"Mirror-Belle!" Ellen called out softly, going into the room and closing the door behind her.

"Nineteen, twenty, twenty-one," came Mirror-Belle's voice.

"I've got you some crisps and some Smarties," said Ellen.

"Be quiet a minute, I'm trying to count." The voice was coming from under the bed. "Twenty-two, twenty-three, twenty-four. The greedy things! This is probably some poor human's life savings."

Ellen lay on her tummy and saw not just Mirror-Belle but a heap of chocolate coins – the kind that are covered in gold paper. An empty little gold net and a pair of gold nail scissors lay beside them.

"Where did

you find those?" she asked.

"Wait till you see what else I've found," said Mirror-Belle, and she ran behind the toy box.

"Not the golden goose, I bet," said Ellen.

"No, but look at this golden hen!" said Mirror-Belle, coming back into view with a little round fluffy Easter chick in her arms. "Unfortunately it seems to be dead," she said as she set it down beside the coins.

"It's not dead, it's just a toy," said Ellen. "I expect Granny and Grandpa were planning to give it to me for Easter – and the coins too. I'll have

to put them back wherever you found them. It's a shame you cut the bag open."

Mirror-Belle wasn't listening. She had

picked up the golden net and taken it back behind the toy box. A moment later she reappeared, dragging it after her. "Look at all this stolen treasure!" she said. Grunting with the effort, she emptied the net.

Ellen gasped in horror as out fell two pairs of gold cufflinks, a watch and a diamond ring.

"I'm sure I recognize this crown," said Mirror-Belle, putting the ring on her head with the diamond at the front. "I seem to remember it went missing from the palace a few years ago. And this clock looks familiar too."

"It's not a clock – it's Granny's best watch. And that's her ring, and Grandpa's cufflinks. Oh, Mirror-Belle, this is terrible! Where did you find them all?"

"I'm not telling you. You'll only

go and put them back," said Mirror-Belle.

"Yes, of course I will. Straight away, before Granny and Grandpa miss them. Go on, Mirror-Belle – you *must* tell me."

"Oh, very well," said Mirror-Belle, who was obviously finding it difficult to resist boasting about her skill as an explorer. "The coins and the golden hen were easy enough to find – they were in a bag under the giants' bed. But the treasure and the golden shears were another matter."

"What golden shears? Oh, you mean the scissors. Where were they?"

"I was just about to tell you. It's a good thing the beanstalk had given me so much climbing practice – though I must say, the white snake was even more difficult."

"What white snake? What are you talking about, Mirror-Belle? Do explain properly!"

"It wasn't actually a snake, I suppose – more of a long, slippery white rope, leading to the giants' treasure chest."

"I think you must mean a light flex," said Ellen. "Right, I'm off."

She scooped up everything that Mirror-Belle had collected.

"Stop! Whose side are you on?" Mirror-Belle protested, but Ellen ignored her.

Making sure to close the door behind her this time, she crept along the landing and into her grandparents' bedroom. She could hear Granny calling her to tea, but she had to put the things back first.

Sure enough, there was a carrier bag under the bed. Inside it were a couple of boxes which must contain Easter eggs. Ellen slipped the fluffy chick and the bag of coins in beside them.

The "white snake" was, as she had suspected, the flex of Granny's bedside lamp. Beside the lamp was a round embroidered jewel box with an unzipped lid. Ellen put the ring, watch and cuff-links inside. She wasn't sure exactly where the scissors belonged but she put them down beside the box and hoped for the best.

Just then she heard footsteps on the stairs.

"Ellen! Where are you? Your tea's getting cold."

Ellen's heart was thumping. If Granny found her here, how would she explain what she was doing? She stood frozen, wondering whether to hide. Then she heard Granny tap at the door of the spare bedroom and go in.

Quickly and quietly, Ellen went downstairs and into the kitchen, where Grandpa was having his tea.

"Your gran's looking for you," he said, and a moment later Granny came in.

"That's funny . . . Oh, there you are, Ellen. Where have you been?"

Ellen muttered something about the bathroom. Granny didn't look too pleased, and Ellen noticed that she was holding the sugar basin in one hand. In her other hand was the jam-jar lid, containing some grape pips and a little bit of cheese.

"What's all this?" said Granny. "Am I not feeding you enough?"

Ellen felt herself go red, but Grandpa said, "Don't scold the lass. I bet she was having a dolls' tea party, weren't you, Ellen?"

Ellen agreed, even though she was too old for that sort of thing. She didn't like lying to her kind grandparents, but it seemed the best way out of a tricky situation.

Granny had made a delicious fruitcake, but Ellen decided against smuggling any of it out to Mirror-Belle. Instead, she would try to persuade her mirror friend to go home.

"You'll have to, Mirror-Belle," she told her after tea. "I can't get you any more food, and Granny's taken your bath back, and . . . well, you must realize that you're not going to find the golden goose."

But Mirror-Belle refused to give up. "Tomorrow I search the garden," she said. "Now, what flavour were those crisps you were telling me about, Ellen? I hope they're smoky dragon ones."

The next day was Easter Sunday. There was a big Easter egg for Ellen on the breakfast table, along with the

fluffy chick and the bag of chocolate
money.

"I'm sorry the bag broke open," said
Granny. "It looked all right in the shop."

"Stop fussing. The lass doesn't mind,"
said Grandpa. He turned to Ellen and
handed her a piece of paper. "Look what
the Easter rabbit left in the garden," he
said.

When she was little Ellen had believed
in the Easter rabbit, but now she knew
that it was Granny and Grandpa who hid
the little eggs in the garden every year,
with clues to help find them. The piece of
paper would be the first clue. She unfolded
it and read, in Grandpa's handwriting:

Red-y? On your marks, get set!
Come and get your feathers wet!

She was rather surprised that Grandpa
couldn't spell the word "ready" – he had
left out the "a" – but was too polite to
mention it.

"You'd better start looking if you want to beat those magpies to it," said Granny. "You know how they love anything shiny."

Ellen was about to run outside when she remembered Mirror-Belle. This could be a good opportunity for her to search the garden and discover that there was no golden goose hidden there after all.

"I'll just put on a cardigan," she said, and went up to her bedroom.

Mirror-Belle was still in her purple silk nightdress, lying in the slipper bed.

"You're interrupting my beauty sleep," she complained when Ellen picked her up. But as soon as she heard the plan she stopped fussing. "I'll need my binoculars," she said, so Ellen gave them to her and she snuggled down into the pocket of Ellen's thick, knitted cardigan.

Once they were outside, Mirror-Belle

peeped out over the top of the pocket. "Where are you going?" she asked Ellen.

"To the bird bath," said Ellen. "This first clue's easy."

Sure enough, on the rim round the bird bath she found seven little eggs. They were all wrapped in red shiny paper, which explained Grandpa's funny spelling of the word "ready".

There was a piece of paper beside the eggs, and on it Ellen read the next clue:

Seven others, bright and blue,
In a nutshell wait for you.

"That's easy too!" she said, and went straight to the half-coconut which Mirror-Belle had wanted as her bath. Inside it were seven blue eggs.

"Excuse me," said Mirror-Belle, "but why are we hunting for eggs? I thought we were supposed to be finding the goose." Then she looked thoughtful. "Of course, it would be a different matter if we found some *golden* eggs. Then I could take one home and hatch it into a golden goose."

"It looks as though the next lot are green," said Ellen, and she read out the clue she had found in the coconut shell:

Small green eggs tell small old man,

"Try and catch us if you can."

Ellen was puzzled at first, and Mirror-Belle said, "That's ridiculous. Eggs can't talk and, anyway, there aren't any small men in giant land."

"I've got it!" Ellen cried. "It must mean one of Grandpa's garden gnomes." One gnome had a wheelbarrow and another was smoking a pipe. Ellen searched around them but couldn't find any eggs. Then, "How stupid of me!" she said, and ran towards the fish pond.

"Slow down! I'm getting pocket-sick!" protested Mirror-Belle.

Standing beside the pond stood a garden

gnome with a fishing rod, and at his feet were seven green eggs.

"That's why the clue says, 'Catch us if you can,'" explained Ellen. "Do you want to hear the next one?"

"If you insist," said Mirror-Belle with a yawn.

So Ellen read it out:

*In the glass you may behold
Seven eggs of shiny gold.*

Mirror-Belle stopped yawning. "The golden eggs!" she cried, and tried to climb out of Ellen's pocket.

"I wonder what 'the glass' means," said Ellen. "I think it could be a pane of the greenhouse."

"Nonsense!" said Mirror-Belle. "It's clearly referring to a mirror."

"But there aren't any mirrors in the

garden," objected Ellen.

"I wouldn't be so sure," said Mirror-Belle, who was much more interested in the egg-hunt now that the next lot of eggs promised to be golden ones. "If you'd only put me down I'm sure that I'd find them in no time."

"All right," said Ellen, "but do be careful." She put Mirror-Belle down at the gnome's feet and said, "I'll see you back here in five minutes." Then she headed for the greenhouse, while Mirror-Belle ran off in the opposite direction.

There weren't any eggs inside the greenhouse. Ellen had just started looking around the outside of it when she heard a triumphant cry: "I've found them!"

Mirror-Belle was standing at the far end of the garden, holding a golden egg above her head. Ellen was surprised at how far she had travelled.

"I'm coming!" she called, and then she saw something else. A magpie was flying down from a tree just above Mirror-Belle. It must have spotted her and decided she could be good to eat.

"Watch out!" Ellen yelled, and started to run. She saw the magpie land and then take off again. Was Mirror-Belle in its beak? She couldn't see.

Ellen reached the spot where she had seen Mirror-Belle. There on the ground was a cluster of golden eggs. She didn't count them, but instead looked round for Mirror-Belle.

"Well? What did you think of the clues?"said Granny. She crossed the lawn and took the piece of paper from Ellen's hand. "That's quite a good one," she said. "Did you spot Grandpa's secret mirror?"

"No," said Ellen. "Where is it?"

Granny pointed at a plant covered in pink flowers. It was a moment before Ellen saw the curved mirror which was standing behind it.

"Another of Grandpa's brainwaves," said Granny. "He was always disappointed that that peony didn't have more flowers, but this way it looks as if it's got twice the amount."

Ellen smiled – not at Grandpa's trick, but because she realized that Mirror-Belle must have disappeared safely into the mirror and not been caught by the magpie after all.

"Did you find all the eggs, then?" asked Granny.

"I think so," said Ellen, and displayed them proudly.

Granny counted them. "There's one missing," she said. "There should be seven of each colour, but you've only found six gold ones." She looked all around the peony and then gave up. "It must be those magpies!" she said.

"Yes, of course," said Ellen, but she knew that even if they found and searched the magpies' nest the missing golden egg would not be in it. Princess Mirror-Belle must have taken it back to mirror land with her. It was only a chocolate egg really, but Ellen couldn't help hoping that it would hatch into a golden goose.

Chapter Three

Prince Precious Paws

"Good, Splodge. Good dog."

For the twentieth time that morning, Ellen picked up the boring-looking stick which lay at her feet. Splodge was gazing up at her with what she called his "Again" look.

"All right, then." Ellen strolled a little way along the lakeside path and then hurled the stick as hard as she could. It landed with a splash in the lake.

In a brown-and-white flash, Splodge was at the water's edge. But there he stopped.

"Go on, Splodge – get it!"

Ellen felt like jumping in herself, the lake looked so cool and inviting under the hot blue sky. But Splodge seemed to have forgotten all about the stick. He was staring into the rippled water and barking. What had he seen? Ellen looked down too. The ripples were clearing now, but all she could see was Splodge's reflection – and her own.

Suddenly the water at their feet started to churn, whirling and splashing as if some huge fish were writhing about in it.

The next second another brown-and-white dog was shaking itself all over Ellen. Splodge barked, and in reply the new dog trotted up and sniffed his bottom. Ellen laughed, then turned to watch

as the two
dogs chased
each other
about on the
grass.

She was
startled by a
voice from
behind her.
"Didn't you
bring a towel?
I'm soaking."

Ellen spun round and there, standing
up to her knees in water, was Mirror-
Belle. She had a dog lead in her hand and
wore a stripy dress just like Ellen's,
except that it was dripping wet.

"Mirror-Belle! What are you doing
here? I thought you only came out of mirrors!" said Ellen. "Though I suppose the
lake *is* a kind of mirror."

"We've been diving for treasure,"

replied Mirror-Belle.

Ellen was puzzled at first. Why had Mirror-Belle said "we" instead of "I"? But then the new dog bounded up to Mirror-Belle, nearly knocking her over. With his paws on her chest, he started to lick her face.

"I didn't know you had a dog too," said Ellen.

"Yes," said Mirror-Belle, in between licks. "His name is Prince Precious Paws."

Ellen thought this was rather a silly name but she was too polite to say so. "He looks just like my dog, Splodge," she said. "Does he like fetching sticks too?"

"Certainly not," said Mirror-Belle, as if she had never heard of such a thing. "Why would he want to fetch sticks when he can find rubies and emeralds?"

"Can he really?"

"Of course. How else do you suppose he helped the little tailor to seek his fortune?"

"What are you talking about? What little tailor? I thought you said he was your dog," said Ellen.

Before Mirror-Belle could launch into an explanation, Splodge – keen for more action and less talk – dropped a new stick at Ellen's feet. She was about to pick it up when Prince Precious Paws seized it and growled.

"You told me he didn't like sticks," said Ellen. She looked accusingly at Mirror-Belle, and Splodge looked accusingly at Prince Precious Paws.

Just then a woman with a pushchair came up to Mirror-Belle.

"You poor thing, did you fall in?" she asked. "I hope your twin sister didn't push you!"

"Ellen's not my twin," said Mirror-Belle indignantly. "I'm a princess and she's just an ordinary girl."

"There's a towel in here somewhere,"

said the woman, rummaging in a bag. "William was going to go paddling but now he's fallen asleep in the pushchair."

As she took out the towel, a ball fell from the bag and rolled towards the water. Both dogs went after it, but Ellen called Splodge back.

"Come, Splodge! Sit!" she said, and Splodge came back obediently and sat at her feet.

Mirror-Belle's dog, however, seized the ball and started chewing it savagely, as if it was a rat he was trying to kill.

"Can you make him bring it back, please?" said the woman. "That's William's new ball and he'd be upset if your dog punctured it."

"I'm surprised you let your child play with such a flimsy toy," said Mirror-Belle. "Personally, I only ever play with a golden ball."

"Just call him back, will you?" said the

woman impatiently.

"Very well." Mirror-Belle raised her voice. "Come, Prince Precious Paws, come!" she cried.

But Prince Precious Paws only growled and rested a paw on the ball.

"He's not very obedient, is he?" said the woman.

"Yes, he is – he's just a bit deaf," said Mirror-Belle. "You see, the tailor who owned him had two other dogs as well. These other two had such terribly loud barks that poor Prince Precious Paws's hearing was affected. So when I said 'Come', he probably thought I was saying 'Hum', and that's why he's making that noise."

As if in agreement, Prince Precious Paws began to growl even louder. It was a fierce sound, not like a hum at all, Ellen thought.

"I've never heard such nonsense," said

the woman. "Look! Now he's ripping poor William's ball apart. I really think you should take him to dog-training classes. Your other dog seems to be very well trained. Are they from the same litter?"

"Of course not," said Mirror-Belle. "Prince Precious Paws is a royal dog. He lives in a kennel lined with dia- monds and pearls. Shall I tell you how he came to be mine?"

"No, thank you," said the woman. "I'm going to take William home before he wakes up and makes a fuss." And, snatching her towel back from Mirror-Belle, she strode off angrily.

Ellen felt embarrassed, and sorry for William, though she supposed that his mother would buy him a new ball. She thought about scolding Mirror-Belle, but perhaps it wasn't her fault that Prince Precious Paws was so badly behaved. Probably his previous owner hadn't brought him up properly.

"You can tell *me* if you like," she said, sitting down on a log by the lake. "How you got your dog, I mean."

Mirror-Belle sat down beside Ellen. Her dress and hair were already much drier, thanks to the hot sun and the woman's towel.

"Prince Precious Paws used to belong to a poor old woman," she began.

"I thought you said he belonged to a little tailor."

"That was later. The little tailor didn't have any dogs to start off with. All he had was a bit of bread and cheese in

a red spotty handkerchief. He was seeking his fortune, you see. But then he met the poor old woman and gave her some of the bread and cheese, and in return for his kindness she gave him three dogs. They all had eyes as big as saucers."

"Are you sure?" asked Ellen.

She couldn't actually see Prince Precious Paws's eyes at that moment, as he was bounding away from them across the grass, pursued by Splodge, but as far as she remembered they were no bigger than Splodge's eyes.

Mirror-Belle ignored the interruption. "Luckily for the tailor," she continued, "the three dogs were all brilliant at finding treasure. They kept finding it, in taverns and caves and all sorts of places, and in the end the tailor arrived at the palace with a great sackful of treasure and asked to marry the King's daughter."

"That's you, isn't it?" said Ellen. "But

you're much too young to get married."

"Exactly," said Mirror-Belle. "So I said I'd take one of the dogs instead."

"What happened to the tailor?" asked Ellen, but she didn't find out, because at that moment they heard some angry shouting and saw Prince Precious Paws bounding towards them with something in his mouth. Behind him ran several people, including a man with glasses and a camera who looked vaguely familiar.

Ellen was relieved to see that her own dog was no longer with Prince Precious Paws but was scrabbling about under a nearby tree, probably looking for yet another stick.

"I'll just see what Splodge is up to," she said, and – feeling rather cowardly – she left Mirror-Belle to face the angry people on her own.

"Your dog's stolen our roast chicken!" she heard the man with the camera complain, and suddenly Ellen recognized him. He was Mr Spalding, a science teacher at her brother Luke's school. Mr Spalding ran a Saturday nature-study club called the Sat Nats. The club was open to adults and teenagers. A couple of the keener members of Luke's class – the ones he called the "geeks" – were members, but Luke himself preferred lying in bed on Saturday mornings.

The other Sat Nats were joining in with Mr Spalding now.

"He knocked over the lemonade."

"He's ruined our picnic."

"I don't call that much of a picnic," replied Mirror-Belle. "One measly roast chicken and a bottle of lemonade! I can assure you, Prince Precious Paws is used to far grander picnics than that. He was probably expecting roast swan and champagne."

A couple of the Sat Nats laughed at this, but not Mr Spalding. "Make him drop the chicken," he ordered.

To Ellen's surprise, Mirror-Belle did say, "Drop it, Prince Precious Paws," in a commanding voice, but Prince Precious Paws took no notice and just started swinging the chicken from side to side.

"He's rather deaf, poor creature," Mirror-Belle explained. "He probably thought I said 'rock it'."

This just made Mr Spalding even angrier. He took a photograph of Prince Precious Paws with the chicken and said he would show it to Mirror-Belle's parents. "Where do you live?" he asked her.

"In the palace, of course," she replied, "and I very much doubt if the guards would let you in. You don't exactly look like royalty. Oh, and whatever you do, don't try picnicking in the palace grounds. That's strictly forbidden."

"I know where she lives, sir," chipped in a teenage Sat Nat. "She's Luke Page's little sister."

Ellen's heart sank.

"I am no one of the sort," Mirror-Belle objected, but Mr Spalding seemed satisfied.

He led the Sat Nats back to the remains of their picnic.

"What an impertinent little man," remarked Princess Mirror-Belle, joining Ellen under the tree.

Ellen knew it would be useless to point out who had actually been the impertinent one. Instead, she fastened Splodge's lead to his collar. "I think I'd better take him home now," she said.

"But we haven't found any treasure yet," protested Mirror-Belle. "I'm convinced that Prince Precious Paws is on the brink of a major discovery."

"Where is he?" asked Ellen.

They both looked around, but Mirror-Belle's dog was nowhere in sight.

"He's lost!" cried Mirror-Belle. "What a catastrophe! I shall have to offer a reward to whoever finds him. Do you think a chest of gold would be enough, or should I offer half my father's kingdom?"

"Why don't we just look for him ourselves?" said Ellen. "He can't have gone far. Let's walk round the lake and call him."

So that is what they did, although Ellen half wished she hadn't suggested it, because she felt so stupid calling out "Prince Precious Paws!" time after time.

"Can't we just call 'Prince'?" she suggested to Mirror-Belle.

"Absolutely not. Prince Precious Paws would never answer to such a common name. In fact, he'd probably run a mile in the other direction."

In the end it was Splodge who picked up the scent. He led the two girls away from the lake along a path which took them over a stile and into a field.

"Oh, no," said Ellen. "We're out of the park now. This is a farm. I hope your dog doesn't chase sheep."

"Only if they're wolves in disguise," said Mirror-Belle, which didn't make Ellen feel much better.

In fact, there were no farm animals in the field, but as they crossed it Ellen heard a loud bleating chorus coming from over the hedge. They climbed another stile and there, huddled in a corner of the next field, was a flock of terrified-looking sheep. Barking as loudly as the sheep were bleating, and making little runs at them, was Prince Precious Paws.

Splodge pulled on the lead and barked. Prince Precious Paws turned and – almost as if to say, "Your turn now"– bounded away into yet another field.

"I hope we don't meet the farmer," said Ellen, keeping Splodge tightly on the lead as they followed Prince Precious Paws. When they caught up with him, he was barking down a hole in a bank of earth.

"It's probably the entrance to an underground cave full of priceless jewels," said Mirror-Belle.

Ellen thought it looked more like the entrance to a rabbit warren, but you never knew. Prince Precious Paws seemed very excited. His tail was wagging and his precious paws were scrabbling away in the earth. Now his head was half inside the hole and he seemed to be tugging at something.

"It could be the handle of a treasure chest," said Mirror-Belle.

"Or maybe some Roman remains," suggested Ellen, growing quite excited herself. "Luke went on a dig near here once and found part of an ancient vase with pictures of dancers on it."

Just then, Prince Precious Paws growled and his head emerged from the hole. He shook the earth from the object in his jaws. It wasn't a treasure chest or a Roman vase.

"It's a dirty old sheep's skull," said Ellen.

"Oh, good," said Mirror-Belle.

"What's so good about it?"

Mirror-Belle thought for a moment and then said, "Haven't you heard of the legendary sheep with the golden fleece? Its bones are obviously buried here. That means that the golden fleece itself must be nearby – probably hanging from a tree and guarded by a fierce dragon.

Prince Precious Paws will find it soon – just wait and see."

"I'm afraid I can't," said Ellen. "I've got to go home for lunch."

She had spotted a gate leading to the road that would take her back home.

"I'll catch up with you as soon as we've found the golden fleece," said

Mirror-Belle, though Ellen rather hoped she wouldn't.

Ellen was just setting off down the road with Splodge when a voice stopped her in her tracks.

"It's that dog again!"

She peeped over the hedge and saw Mr Spalding climbing over the stile into the field, followed by his troop of poor hungry Sat Nats.

"He's still not on the lead!"

"What's that he's got?"

"It's a sheep's skull, isn't it, Mr Spalding? He must have killed one of the sheep and eaten it!"

Ellen didn't stop to hear more, but hurried on with Splodge. It was quite a long walk and she was going to be late for lunch. They were just coming to the place where the road bent sharply and led towards the village when she heard footsteps. She turned and saw Mirror-Belle running towards her. Prince Precious Paws was on the lead at last, and was tugging her along at an amazing speed.

"Can't stop, must fly," Mirror-Belle greeted Ellen as they overtook her and went careering round the bend.

"Watch out, that's a dangerous corner!" Ellen called after them.

When she and Splodge rounded the same bend a minute later, there was no sign of Mirror-Belle or her dog. Although they'd been going so fast, Ellen hadn't expected them to be out of sight already. But then she noticed the mirror by the roadside. It was there so that drivers could see what was coming round the corner. Mirror-Belle and Prince Precious Paws must have disappeared into it.

*

The next day, Luke was practising his electric guitar in his bedroom when the doorbell rang. No one else seemed to be in, so reluctantly he went to the door and was surprised to see his science teacher standing outside.

"Good afternoon, Luke. Are either of your parents in?"

"No, they're not," said Luke, feeling suddenly guilty, as if his teacher somehow knew he hadn't started on his science homework yet.

"Don't worry, this isn't about school," said Mr Spalding, and Luke relaxed a little. He guessed that his teacher must be trying to recruit new members for the Sat Nats.

"I'd really like to join your club, Mr Spalding, but I'm usually rather busy on Saturday mornings, doing my homework, and . . . er . . . taking the dog for a walk."

Hearing his favourite word, Splodge

appeared in the hallway, his lead in his mouth.

"Here's the culprit himself," said Mr Spalding. "That dog is badly in need of training."

Luke started to protest, but Mr Spalding reached into his pocket and handed him two photographs.

"Stealing food and running about off the lead on a sheep farm. Would you call that the behaviour of a well-trained dog?"

Luke studied the photographs. One showed a brown-and-white dog with what looked like a roast chicken in his jaws. In the other picture, the same dog was proudly resting his paw on a sheep skull.

Luke frowned, but then his face cleared.

"You've made a mistake, Mr Spalding. You see, we call our dog Splodge because of the brown splodges on his side and over his eye."

"Exactly. And there they are in the pictures – there's no denying it."

"But Splodge's marks are on his right side and over his left eye – look, you can see. This dog's marks are on his left side and over his right eye."

Mr Spalding looked from the photographs to Splodge and back again. "You're quite right . . . But the girl he was with looked just like your sister . . . It's most extraordinary."

"Don't worry, Mr Spalding. We all make mistakes sometimes," said Luke graciously.

"Well, I do apologize. And perhaps I should apologize to you, old chap," said Mr Spalding, patting Splodge rather timidly on the head.

Luke wondered if Splodge knew he had been wrongly accused. Maybe he even knew who the mystery dog was. But Splodge just gazed up at Mr Spalding with his usual trusting expression. Whatever he knew, he was keeping quiet about it.

Chapter Four

Which Witch?

"Two witches flew out on a moonlit night.

Their laughs were loud and their eyes were
  bright.

Their chins and their noses were pointed
  and long.

They shared the same broom and they
  sang the same song.

Their hats and their cloaks were as black
  as pitch,

And nobody knew which witch was which."

It was Halloween. Ellen, dressed up as
a witch, was practising the poem she
was planning to go round reciting with

her friend Katy.

Most of Ellen's other friends were going out trick-or-treating, but Ellen's mum disapproved of that. She said that in Scotland, where she grew up, children had to recite a poem or tell a joke to earn their Halloween treats. So that was what Ellen and Katy were going to do. It was called guising.

Downstairs, Mum was teaching the piano. One of her star pupils was playing a fast piece whose tune kept going very low and then very high. It reminded Ellen of a witch swooping and soaring on her broomstick, and made her feel excited.

The phone rang. Ellen answered it, and a snuffly Katy said, "It's so unfair. My mum won't let me go out, just because my cold's got worse."

"Oh, poor you," said Ellen, but it was herself she really felt sorry for. As she put the phone down, all her excitement vanished. What was she going to do? She didn't feel like going out on her own, and anyway the poem was supposed to be recited by two identical witches. But now it was too late to ask anyone else to go with her. She would just have to stay at home. What a waste of all the trouble she had taken over her costume — sewing silver stars on to the cloak, spraying glitter on the hat and carving a face out of her pumpkin lantern. She glanced wistfully at herself in the mirror.

"What's the matter? Don't tell me you've lost your cat," came a familiar voice, and a witchy Princess Mirror-Belle stepped out of the mirror, shedding glitter and flourishing her wand.

For once, Ellen was delighted to see her. "What good timing!" she greeted Mirror-Belle. "Now we can go guising together!"

"Disguising is not for the likes of me," said Mirror-Belle. "Your costume may be a disguise, but I really *am* a witch."

"I said *guising*, not disguising," said Ellen, "and anyway, how can you be a witch when you're always telling me you're a princess?"

"Of course I'm a princess," replied Mirror-Belle. "But a wicked ogre has turned me into a witch. A *royal* witch, of course," she added hastily.

"Why did he do that?"

"Because my golden ball landed in his garden and he saw me climbing over his wall to get it back."

"If you're a real witch, can you actually fly that broomstick?" asked Ellen hopefully. Mirror-Belle was holding a small twiggy broomstick just the same as her own.

"Unfortunately, the rotten wizard refused to give me a cat, and everyone knows that a broomstick won't fly without a cat on it. I was hoping that I could borrow your cat, but you seem to have let it escape."

"I never had one," said Ellen. "Anyway, Mirror-Belle, do please come guising with me. I'll teach you the poem, and then we can go round the houses and people will give us lots of goodies."

Mirror-Belle's eyes lit up at the mention of goodies and, after a quick rehearsal of the poem, she followed Ellen downstairs. The impressive sounds of Mum's star pupil were still drifting out of the sitting room.

Ellen found them each a carrier bag. "These are to collect the goodies," she explained. "Mum says we're only to go to people we know and only in this block."

They stepped out into the night.

"Let's start here," said Mirror-Belle, marching up to the house next door.

"No, number 17's been empty since the Johnsons moved out," Ellen told her. "We'll go to the Elliots'."

Mr and Mrs Elliot were the elderly couple who lived two doors along and always had a supply of old-fashioned sweets like pear drops and humbugs and bullseyes.

Mrs Elliot opened the door. She pretended to be scared. "Oh, help!' I'd better let you in quickly, before you turn me into a toad," she said.

"Yes, that would be a good idea," Mirror-Belle agreed.

Mrs Elliot showed them into the cosy front room, where her husband was sitting in an armchair by the fire.

Ellen and Mirror-Belle recited their poem, and Ellen was pleased at how well Mirror-Belle remembered it.

"And nobody knew which witch was which," they finished up. At least, it was supposed to be the end, but Mirror-Belle carried on with another two lines:

"But one of the two was in fancy dress
    While the other was really a royal princess."

Mr Elliot chuckled, and Mrs Elliot said, "You've definitely earned your bullseyes."

"I'd rather have some newts' eyes, if you don't mind," said Mirror-Belle. "They're better for spells."

Mrs Elliot just laughed. She took down a big glass jar from the mantelpiece and began to pour some of the striped sweets into Mirror-Belle's carrier bag.

"These don't look like eyes to me," Mirror-Belle complained. "They're just boiled sweets. How are we supposed to do any magic with them?"

Ellen glared at her, but the Elliots laughed again, as if Mirror-Belle had been performing another party piece.

Mr Elliot beckoned them over and handed them two fifty-pence pieces.

"Oh, I see," said Mirror-Belle. "You're expecting us to go to the eye shop ourselves." Then she studied her coin. "I don't think any decent

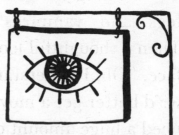

eye shop would accept this," she said. "The writing is back to front."

"Stop being so cheeky," Ellen muttered, but Mr Elliot roared with laughter and said, "This beats the telly any day."

When they were back outside, Ellen ticked Mirror-Belle off again. "I know the Elliots thought it was funny, but other people might not," she said. "And I don't want to get Katy into trouble. Remember that people probably think you're her."

"But it's so puzzling," said Mirror-Belle. "What do witches want with sweets and money? Surely we should be collecting things like frogs' legs and vampires' teeth?"  Then a thoughtful look crossed her face. "Oh, I understand," she said. "Well, we'd better get a move on. We're going to need a huge amount of sweets."

Ellen didn't really see why, but she wasn't in the mood for listening to a long, fanciful explanation, so she was relieved to see Mirror-Belle striding up the path of the next house and ringing on the bell.

An hour or so later, their carrier bags were full of sweets, biscuits, fruit and money.

"Shall we go back to my house?" Ellen suggested to Mirror-Belle, who had been remarkably well behaved – apart from adding the extra two lines to the poem every time they recited it.

"I don't think we'll need to do that," said Mirror-Belle mysteriously.

Before Ellen could ask what she meant, she was striding off again.

"Where are you going?" asked Ellen, trying to catch up.

"In here," said Mirror-Belle, and

pointed her wand at the doors of the mini-supermarket at the end of the road. The doors swung open, as they always did, but she turned and gave Ellen a triumphant look as if she had performed some magic.

Mirror-Belle took a trolley. She dumped her wand and broomstick in it and hung her lantern and carrier bag on the hook at the back. Then she pushed it swiftly up the first aisle to the meat counter at the far end of the shop. Ellen had a horrible feeling that she was going to start demanding newts' eyes and frogs' legs, but instead Mirror-Belle turned her back on the

counter and began to recite the poem at the top of her voice.

There weren't many customers in the shop and, to Ellen's relief, no one took much notice. But her relief faded when Mirror-Belle, having finished her version of the poem on a note of triumph, pushed her trolley down the next aisle and started filling it with sweets.

"You can't just take all of those!" Ellen protested, as Mirror-Belle threw in a dozen bags of toffees.

"I agree it would have been polite of someone to offer them to us – not to mention loading the trolley – but unfortunately there's not a servant in sight," said Mirror-Belle, emptying the shelves of liquorice allsorts and reaching for the jelly babies. "It would be quicker if you'd help me," she added.

Ellen tried to think of something to say that would stop Mirror-Belle, but she knew from experience how difficult this was. In any case, the trolley was nearly full now and Mirror-Belle seemed satisfied with her haul.

"Come on," she said, and made her way to one of the checkouts. But instead of stopping and taking the sweets out, she sailed on through.

"Stop!" cried Ellen.

Mirror-Belle was about to push the trolley outside when a shop assistant ran after her and grabbed it.

Ellen felt terrified. What if they were both arrested for shoplifting?

"You haven't paid for this lot, have you?" said the assistant.

"Certainly not," replied Mirror-Belle. "Has it escaped your attention that this is Halloween and that Ellen and I are guising?"

"Not in here, you're not," the shop assistant said firmly.

Mirror-Belle turned to Ellen. "Shall we turn this rude servant into a black beetle?" she suggested.

The shop assistant ignored her and steered the trolley firmly back to the checkout.

"You either pay for them or put them back," he said.

"It's extremely lucky for you that my wand is buried under all the sweets," Mirror-Belle told him. "Poor Ellen here isn't a real witch like me, so she can't do the black-beetle spell."

Ellen could see that Mirror-Belle was just making the assistant angrier and she was scared that he might phone the police. She had to make Mirror-Belle see sense!

"Listen, Mirror-Belle," she said. "We did collect quite a lot of money. If you're so keen for more sweets, perhaps we can buy some of them."

Mirror-Belle sighed. "Very well," she said, "if you think it will stop the servants rioting."

They had enough money for five bags of toffees, four each of liquorice allsorts and jelly babies, and six packets of chewing gum.

"But we'll be sick if we eat all these as well as the sweets and chocolates people gave us," Ellen objected as they left the shop.

"Eat them, did you say? *Eat* them?" Mirror-Belle laughed, as if the idea were absurd. "Where would we live if we ate them?"

"What are you talking about?"

"I'm afraid you're not very well informed about witches, Ellen. Didn't you know that they always live in houses made of sweets?"

Ellen thought about this. "I know that

the witch in 'Hansel and Gretel' had a house of sweets – or was it gingerbread? – but I can't think of any others."

"Where will we build it, I wonder," mused Mirror-Belle, ignoring Ellen and marching back the way they had come. "I know! In the garden of that empty house."

"Mirror-Belle, don't be silly. We haven't got nearly enough sweets to build a house. And anyway, how would we stick them all together?"

"Chewing gum!" said Mirror-Belle, popping a piece into her mouth. "Ah, here we are."

They had reached the empty house, and she opened the tall side gate which led into the overgrown back garden. Ellen followed her nervously.

"Oh, how thoughtful of somebody," said Mirror-Belle, pointing at a large shed in the corner of the garden. "Someone's built it for us already. We'll only need to decorate it."

At first Ellen just watched as Mirror-Belle started to stick jelly babies round one of the shed windows. But it did look rather good fun and soon she was joining in.

"Black, white, pink, yellow,"

she muttered,
as she created a
coloured pattern with liquorice allsorts round the other window. She was standing back to admire the effect when the garden gate creaked and began to open.

"Someone's coming!" she hissed. She pulled Mirror-Belle behind the shed, but couldn't stop her peeping round the edge.

"I think it's the delivery men, come to furnish our new house," said Mirror-Belle. "But surely we don't need two televisions?"

She hadn't lowered her voice, but luckily it was drowned by a crash and a curse from the garden.

Ellen couldn't resist a peep herself. Although the garden was dark, she could make out two men, one carrying a television and another picking up a second television from the ground. Both of them were wearing balaclava helmets over their heads, so that only their eyes showed. They didn't look like delivery men to Ellen, more like burglars who were hiding stolen goods. But she didn't risk whispering this fear to Mirror-Belle, in case they heard her.

One of the men had opened the shed door and must have been putting the televisions inside, while the other went back through the gate and then reappeared with a large square object covered in a sheet. Probably a stolen picture, thought Ellen.

A sudden idea struck her. If she and Mirror-Belle climbed over the low wall into her own garden, they could get into her house through the back door and phone the police. With a finger over her lips, she pointed at the wall and then beckoned to Mirror-Belle.

Ellen was already over the wall when she realized that Mirror-Belle wasn't following her.

"It's a witch!" she heard one of the men say, and, "Don't be daft, it's a kid," from the other. And then came Mirror-Belle's voice – loud, clear and bossy as ever: "Don't just dump that on the floor. Aren't you going to hang it on the wall?"

Instead of following Ellen, Mirror-Belle must have gone to check what sort of a job the "delivery men" were doing.

Ellen stood frozen, uncertain whether to join Mirror-Belle or run home for help. Then she heard one of the men again. This time he was talking to Mirror-Belle.

"I do apologize, madam. Just step inside and wait while we fetch our tool-box."

The next sounds came quickly. A slam, a metallic clink, some bashing and an angry "Let me out! What is the meaning of this?" from Mirror-Belle. Then footsteps and the creak of the garden gate. The men had locked Mirror-Belle in the shed and escaped!

But *had* they both escaped? Ellen didn't dare investigate by herself. Instead, she ran through her own garden and into the house through the back door.

"Help! Help!" she cried.

Dad came out of the kitchen, followed by Mum and Luke.

"What's the matter? Did a skeleton jump out at you?" Dad asked jokily.

"The burglars have locked Mirror-Belle in the shed next door!" shrieked Ellen. "And now they're getting away!"

Mum and Dad still seemed to think this was some Halloween prank. It was Luke who ran to the front window.

"Two men are getting into a van," he reported. "And they're wearing masks, or hoods, or something."

"Take down the number," said Dad, and reached for the phone to call the police.

Mum made Ellen sit down and drink some hot sweet tea "for shock".

When Ellen protested, "But we must go back next door! Mirror-Belle's trapped! We've got to rescue her!" Dad said, "Not till the police arrive." Ellen knew he thought Mirror-Belle was just an imaginary friend.

"Where's Katy?" said Mum suddenly.

"She's all right. She's at home," said Ellen, but Mum phoned Katy's parents just the same.

"That's strange. She's in bed with a cold," Mum said, sounding relieved but puzzled.

"Yes . . . she couldn't come, but then Mirror-Belle . . ." Ellen began, but a ring at the bell interrupted her explanation. It was the police.

Katy was back at school on Monday. Like the rest of Ellen's class, she had read in the paper about Ellen's discovery of the shed full of stolen goods, and of how the burglars had been caught thanks to Luke getting the number of their van.

"Just think! If only I hadn't had that cold I'd be in the paper too," she said.

"But if you'd come with me instead of Mirror-Belle, we wouldn't have gone to number 17."

"Did the police find Mirror-Belle as well as all the televisions?" asked Katy. Unlike Ellen's family, she believed in Mirror-Belle, who had once come to their school.

"No," said Ellen. "You see, the men hadn't just stolen televisions. When we were there they were hiding away something else. I thought it was a great big picture, but it wasn't."

"What was it, then?" asked Katy.

"It was a mirror," said Ellen.

Chapter Five

The Princess Test

"I hope you haven't put spaghetti on that shopping list," said Ellen to her brother, Luke. "Or mince. Or tinned tomatoes."

"Don't worry, bossyboots, we're not going to have spag bol again." Luke crumpled the shopping list and stuffed it into his pocket. "I'm going to make chicken vindaloo."

"What's that?"

"It's this really hot curry."

Ellen wasn't sure that really hot curry would be the right sort of supper for Mum, who had just had her appendix out. But it was a relief that it wouldn't be yet more spaghetti bolognese, which was what Dad had cooked just about every night of the week Mum had been in hospital. It used to be Ellen's favourite food, but now she didn't mind if she never ate it again.

Mum was coming home today; Dad had gone to fetch her from the hospital. He had warned Ellen and Luke that she would still be a bit weak after the operation and that they would have to be extra helpful. So Luke had agreed to do the shopping and cook the supper, and Ellen was going to make the bedroom look nice for Mum's return.

Luke went out, slamming the front door, and Ellen took the cleaning things upstairs. She had decided to make Mum a "Welcome Home" card and pick some flowers from the garden. But first she really ought to do the boring housework-y things.

She straightened the duvet on the bed and then picked up the yellow duster.

Dust was such funny stuff, she thought to herself. No one actually sprinkled it on the furniture; it just appeared from nowhere. "And what *is* it exactly?" she wondered out loud as she began to dust Mum's dressing table.

"What is what?" came a voice.

"Dust," Ellen replied automatically, and then, "Mirror-Belle! It's you!"

"Yes, though why you should be asking me questions about dust I have no idea. I've never even *seen* dust," said Mirror-Belle in a superior voice.

There were three mirrors on Mum's dressing table: a big one in the middle and, joined on to it, two smaller ones which slanted inwards. Mirror-Belle was

leaning out of
the middle mirror. "You
seem to forget that I'm
a princess, not a maid," she said.

"Oh, no, you're not," came another
voice, and Ellen was amazed to see a second Mirror-Belle – at least, that was
what she looked like – sticking a hand
out of the left-hand mirror and wagging
a finger at the first Mirror-Belle. "You
know very well that you're a maid. You're
my maid." She turned to Ellen and said,

"She's always disguising herself as me. Once, when we were on a journey to another kingdom, she made me swap clothes and horses with her, and when we got there she managed to kid everyone that she was the princess, so I was sent to feed the geese."

"What a pack of lies," said the first Mirror-Belle, who had slithered out of the mirror and was swinging her legs to the ground. "She's got it the wrong way round. *She's* the maid and *I'm* the one who had to feed the geese. But of course my sweet singing soon made everyone realize that I was the real princess."

"You've got a voice like a crow," said the second Mirror-Belle, beginning to slither out herself.

The first one tried to push her back, and Ellen cried, "Be careful or you'll break the glass!"

"Stop this commotion at once!" came another voice. A third identical girl was reaching out from the right-hand mirror and had picked up Mum's silver-backed hairbrush. "Now, you two lazybones, whose turn is it to brush my hair today?"

"Are *you* the real Mirror-Belle?" asked Ellen.

"Naturally – don't you recognize me?" said the newest Mirror-Belle, but the other two said, "Nonsense," and, "She's Ethel, the kitchen maid."

"Well, you all look exactly the same to me," said Ellen. "And none of you looks specially like a princess. You don't really look like maids either. At least, I suppose you have all got dusters, but you haven't got caps and aprons. Really, you all look just like me."

All three Mirror-Belles had a complicated explanation for this, but since they all talked at once Ellen couldn't make out what the different explanations were, and she didn't really care.

"I give up," she said. "In any case, does it really matter who's who?"

"Of course it does!" said all three mirror girls together.

This at least was something they were agreed on.

"I know!" said the first one. "You must give us a test, Ellen, to find out which is the true princess."

"What sort of a test?" Ellen asked.

"Well, if you had a frog, you could see which of us could kiss it and turn it into a prince," said the second girl.

"Or we could lie on the bed and see who could detect if there was a pea under the mattress," suggested the third one. "Only a real princess could do that."

"I haven't got a frog," said Ellen, "and I've only just made the bed. I don't want you all messing it up again." In any case, she had bad memories of pea-detection and frog-kissing. Mirror-Belle had tried these things out in a shop once and got them both into trouble.

Still, Ellen quite liked the idea of a test.

"I'll think of something," she told them. "But first, I must be able to tell you apart. Just stand still a minute."

She took one of Mum's lipsticks from a little drawer in the dressing table. She wrote a big L on the forehead of the Mirror-Belle who had come out of the left mirror. On the foreheads of the other two she wrote R and M, for right and middle.

"What is the test going to be?" they all kept clamouring.

"It's a quiz," said Ellen, "and I'm the quizmaster."

She was enjoying herself. For once she was the one in charge, instead of being ordered about by Mirror-Belle. But it was going to be hard thinking up the questions.

"I'll just put Mum's lipstick back in the drawer," she said, and that made her wonder what a princess would call her own mother. She wouldn't say "Mum", like an ordinary person, surely? But "Your Majesty" didn't sound quite right either. This was something that a real princess would know the answer to, and would make a good quiz question.

"Question number one: what do you call your mother?"

They all answered at once, so Ellen made them take turns.

"Your Mumjesty," said Mirror-Belle L.

"Queen Mother," said Mirror-Belle R.

"O Most Royal Madam whom I Respect and Obey without Question," said Mirror-Belle M.

Ellen couldn't decide which of these sounded right, so she moved on to another question. A dog barking in the distance made her think about Mirror-Belle's dog, Prince Precious Paws, and that gave her another idea.

"What would a real princess give to her dog for his birthday?" she asked.

This time she made them answer in a different order.

"A golden bone," said Mirror-Belle R.

"How common! An emerald-studded collar would be a far more suitable gift," said Mirror-Belle M.

"What's so special about that?" asked Mirror-Belle L. "I'm planning to give Prince Precious Paws something magical — an  invisible lead, which will make *him* invisible when I put it on him. In fact, I've brought one for your dog, Splodge, too. Here it is." She reached out to Ellen as if she were handing her something.

The other two Mirror-Belles became very indignant at this.

"She's an impostor!" cried Mirror-Belle R. "Besides, I've brought you a *far* better invisible present. It's . . . um . . . a spoon that will change whatever you're eating into your favourite food."

Ellen didn't really believe in the invisible spoon, but she pretended to take it and said, "I wish I'd had this when Dad was doing the cooking."

"Invisible spoons are two a penny," said Mirror-Belle M scornfully. "I've brought you . . . er . . . some invisible pyjamas. If you wear them at night, all your dreams will come true."

All three Mirror-Belles were crowding round her, offering her more and more invisible things, and Ellen was losing the feeling of being the one in charge. The quiz seemed to have turned into a boasting session.

"And here's an invisible clock . . ." began Mirror-Belle M.

"Stop!" cried Ellen.

The invisible clock had reminded her that Mum would be back from hospital soon. She would never get the bedroom ready at this rate. Not on her own, anyway, and the three Mirror-Belles were so eager to prove that they were not maids they would never agree to help. Unless . . .

Suddenly, Ellen had an idea. "I've thought of a test," she said. "I've just remembered that there is a . . . a sort of fairy imprisoned in the furniture in this room and only a true princess will be able to set her free."

The Mirror-Belles started opening drawers, but Ellen stopped them.

"No, the fairy's not in a drawer or cupboard. She's in the actual *wood* of the furniture. You have to rub the wood to get her out."

"Oh, a wood nymph, you mean," said Mirror-Belle R. "Why didn't you say so before?" and she immediately began to rub the dressing table with her duster.

"She might be in the mantelpiece . . . or in the wood of the bedside table," suggested Ellen, and the other two Mirror-Belles set to work with their dusters.

They were all rubbing furiously. Soon there was not a speck of dust to be seen, and the furniture was shiny bright.

"You've all failed that test," Ellen said. "The wood nymph doesn't seem to realize that one of you is a princess."

Once again, all three Mirror-Belles started on explanations for this, but Ellen interrupted them. "I've thought of a different test," she said. "Well, it's more of a quest than a test. Down in the garden there is a talking flower. But it will only talk if it's picked and put into a vase of water by a true princess."

The three girls ran to the bedroom door, eager to be downstairs and out in the garden. Ellen was suddenly afraid that they would pick every single flower, so she called out after them, "The flower will only talk if the princess picks no more than five flowers altogether."

While the Mirror-Belles picked the flowers, Ellen filled a vase with water and put it on Mum's gleaming bedside table. She was just making a start on her "Welcome Home" card when the Mirror-Belles charged back into the room and thrust their flowers into the vase. The flowers looked very pretty but they were completely silent.

"I expect the magic flower is too shy to talk

to me when there are two maids in the room," said one of the Mirror-Belles, and the other two said, "To *me*, you mean."

Just then Ellen heard the front door bang. Help! Was Dad back with Mum already? The room did look really nice now, but how was she going to get rid of the three Mirror-Belles? She was sure Mum wouldn't want them all in her bedroom when she was trying to rest.

"I'm back!" came Luke's voice.

Of course – she should have recognized the way he slammed the door. Still, Mum would be back any minute now.

"Give us another test, Ellen," the Mirror-Belles were demanding, and suddenly Ellen knew what to do.

"All right," she said, "but this one is really difficult. You've given me all these invisible presents, which is very nice of you, but I'm sure that only a real princess would know how to make *herself* invisible."

As Ellen closed her eyes and counted to a hundred, she remembered the very first time she had ever met Mirror-Belle. That time, Mirror-Belle had tricked her by blindfolding her with toilet paper and then disappearing into the bathroom mirror. This time, it was Ellen who was tricking Mirror-Belle. She felt a bit guilty and wondered where she had learned to make up so many stories. But of course she knew the answer really – it was from Mirror-Belle.

As she had hoped, when she got to a hundred and opened her eyes, the room was empty. She was very careful indeed not to steal a glance at the mirrors on the dressing table, in case the mirror princesses (or maids) reappeared. Instead, she lay on her tummy on the floor and carried on with the "Welcome Home" card.

She had just finished it when she heard the front door opening again.

Ellen jumped to her feet and ran downstairs into the arms of the person she most wanted to see in the whole world.

"Come and look at your bedroom, Mum!" she said.

"Don't tire her out," said Dad, but Mum laughed and let herself be tugged upstairs by Ellen.

She admired the card and the flowers and the neatly made bed. "And what shining surfaces!" she said. "I never knew you were so good at housework, Ellen! It's a real treat to come home to this."

Ellen wished that Mirror-Belle could hear. She was the one who deserved most of the praise.

"I wanted you to have a nice treat to come home to," she muttered to Mum.

Mum hugged her again and said, "Do you know what the biggest treat is? Seeing you!"

A strong spicy smell was wafting into the room.

"That smells even better than spaghetti bolognese," said Mum, and together they went downstairs.

Princess Mirror-Belle

Julia Donaldson

Illustrated by Lydia Monks

Don't miss the first collection of stories all about mischievous Mirror-Belle and her friend, Ellen.

The two friends have lots of exciting adventures – but they always seem to end up with Ellen getting into trouble and Mirror-Belle escaping . . .

POEMS BY
JULIA DONALDSON
Illustrated by Nick Sharratt

When my friends come home with me
They never want to stay for tea
Because of Mum's peculiar meals
Like strawberries with jellied eels.
You should see her lick her lips
And sprinkle sugar on the chips,
Then pass a cup of tea to you
And ask, 'One salt or two?'

Whoops-a-daisy,
That's my crazy
Mayonnaisy Mum

Come meet Crazy Mayonnaisy Mum and lots of other
wonderful characters in this fantastic collection of
lively poems. It is packed with number rhymes, story
poems, noisy rhymes, scenes from everyday life, and
some more reflective poems too. Have fun.